Flicka, Ricka, Dicka
and the
NEW DOTTED DRESSES

MAJ LINDMAN

ALBERT WHITMAN & COMPANY
Morton Grove, Illinois

The Snipp, Snapp, Snurr Books
Snipp, Snapp, Snurr and the Buttered Bread
Snipp, Snapp, Snurr and the Gingerbread
Snipp, Snapp, Snurr and the Red Shoes
Snipp, Snapp, Snurr and the Reindeer
Snipp, Snapp, Snurr and the Yellow Sled
Snipp, Snapp, Snurr Learn to Swim

The Flicka, Ricka, Dicka Books
Flicka, Ricka, Dicka Bake a Cake
Flicka, Ricka, Dicka and the Big Red Hen
Flicka, Ricka, Dicka and the Little Dog
Flicka, Ricka, Dicka and the New Dotted Dresses
Flicka, Ricka, Dicka and the Three Kittens
Flicka, Ricka, Dicka and Their New Friend

Library of Congress Cataloging-in-Publication Data
Lindman, Maj.
Flicka, Ricka, Dicka and the new dotted dresses/
written & illustrated by Maj Lindman.
p.   cm.
Summary: Three little girls get their new red dresses all dirty
while helping an old woman with her chores.
ISBN 0-8075-2494-8
[1. Helpfulness—Fiction. 2. Triplets—Fiction.
3. Sweden—Fiction.] I. Title. II. Title: New Dotted Dresses.
PZ7.L659Flgn 1994   94-15282
[E]—dc20   CIP   AC

The text is set in Futura Book and Bookman Light Italic.

A Flicka, Ricka, Dicka Book

The three little girls looked very much alike.

Flicka, Ricka, and Dicka were three little girls who lived in Sweden. They looked very much alike. They had blue eyes and yellow curls, and they always wore dresses that were just alike.

One summer morning their mother said, "I have made new dotted dresses for you. Would you like to wear them today?"

Flicka said, "Oh, yes! I like to wear new dresses."

Ricka said, "I love red dresses with big white dots."

Dicka said, "These dresses have white collars, too!"

When the three little girls had put on their new dotted dresses, they ran outdoors to play.

Be sure to keep your new dresses clean!" Mother called as they ran through the meadow toward the woods.

Flicka and Dicka picked daisies. Ricka tried to catch a butterfly, but it flew just ahead of her. Ricka ran after it.

"We must remember to keep our new dotted dresses clean," said Flicka.

"Perhaps we had better take our flowers back to Mother," said Dicka.

But Ricka was running after the butterfly. On and on she ran. The sun was shining, the birds were singing, the daisies were blooming everywhere, and the three little girls were very happy in their new dotted dresses.

But Ricka was running after the butterfly.

Suddenly Ricka stopped. Just where the meadow met the woods was a path. A little old woman was walking slowly along it. She carried a load of firewood on her back, and she was wearing an old-fashioned hood. When she saw the three little girls, she smiled.

Flicka, Ricka, and Dicka greeted her. "Good morning," they said. "May we help you with your heavy load?"

The little old woman smiled again. She let the load of firewood slip to the ground.

"Thank you, little girls," she said. "I am taking this wood to my cottage. The wood is very heavy, and I am tired. You are most kind."

A little old woman was walking slowly along the path.

When each little girl had taken all the wood she could hold, there was none left for the little old woman to carry. Flicka walked beside her on her right, and Ricka walked beside her on her left. Dicka walked close behind.

Through the woods they went, to the little old woman's cottage.

"I am Flicka. These are my two sisters, Ricka and Dicka. We have on new dotted dresses," said Flicka.

"Oh!" replied the little old woman. "Do you think you should be carrying that wood? Perhaps you will get your new dotted dresses dirty."

"Oh, Mother has always taught us to help people," said Ricka.

Through the woods they went, to the little old woman's cottage.

So Flicka, Ricka, Dicka, and the little old woman walked on through the woods. When they came to the end of the path, they saw a red cottage. It had green shutters, and flowers were growing everywhere.

"What a pretty little house!" cried Ricka as she put her load of wood near the door.

"Can we help you any other way?" asked Flicka.

Dicka thought about Mother and their new dotted dresses. "Perhaps we had better go home now," she said. But as she spoke she heard a loud "Moo-moo-moo!" The sound was coming from behind the cottage.

"That's Masie," said the little old woman.

They saw a red cottage.

Masie is my cow," she explained as she seated herself on the doorstep. "You may call me Aunt Helma. I am very tired, and there is so much to do. I need fresh water from the spring. The chickens should be fed, and I need potatoes for supper. They are down in the cellar."

Flicka ran right to the spring. Soon she returned with two big pails of water that splashed on her dotted dress with every step.

Ricka went down to the cellar and brought up the potatoes in a big basket.

Dicka fed the chickens. "They are all white but one, aren't they, Aunt Helma?" she asked.

"Yes, Dicka," was the answer, "but the brown one lays the most eggs."

"Masie is my cow," she explained.

Aunt Helma, may we milk Masie?" asked Flicka.

She smiled. "You may try," she said. "Masie is in the barn just behind the cottage. Here is the pail."

Flicka, Ricka, and Dicka ran to the barn.

Ricka seated herself on a little stool and began to milk. When she had filled the pail, she carried it to the cottage while Dicka swept the floor of the barn.

Flicka carried sweet-smelling hay to the cow. "Here is your supper, Masie," she said. "I hope you enjoy it. Aunt Helma was much too tired to milk you. Now good night."

Then back to the cottage they ran.

"Here is your supper, Masie," she said.

We must feed the pig," said Flicka. "Aunt Helma has his supper here in the pail."

She ran toward the pigpen and pushed open the gate. She was about to empty the bucket into the trough when she heard Ricka and Dicka cry, "The pig is out!"

Out of the pen, across the yard, and through the flowers ran the pig, with Flicka, Ricka, and Dicka close behind. Flicka still carried the pig's supper in the pail.

Dicka fell down, but Flicka and Ricka ran on.

Aunt Helma stood watching. How she laughed when Ricka finally caught the pig!

Across the yard ran the pig.

When the pig was back in the pen and Aunt Helma herself had fastened the gate, she said, "Flicka, Ricka, and Dicka, you must be hungry. Come now. You may each have a cup of Masie's fresh milk. Perhaps I can find some cookies, too."

She put a cloth on the table, and soon the three little girls sat down.

"My, how good this milk is," said Flicka as she drank every drop.

"I like these cookies!" said Ricka.

Perhaps Dicka was looking at the cookies. Perhaps she was only tired. But in a moment her milk had spilled all over her dress, her socks, and her shoes.

Soon the three little girls sat down.

Oh, my new dotted dress is covered with milk," said Dicka, sobbing.

"Mine is all dirty, too," said Flicka. "Now we really must go, Aunt Helma. It is almost dark. I'm afraid Mother will be anxious."

"Thank you for all you have done, my dears," said Aunt Helma. "Come again soon."

Then off through the woods ran the three little girls. It grew dark. "If we climb over this fence," said Flicka, "we'll get home much sooner."

Over the fence climbed Dicka, still crying. But Ricka's dress caught on the fence as she climbed, and she tore a big hole in it.

Ricka's dress caught on the fence.

Oh, dear," sobbed Ricka. "Now I've torn my new dotted dress."

But on they ran, through the woods, across the meadow, right to the door where Mother stood—looking and waiting.

When she saw her three little girls, she caught them in her arms. "Oh! Your dirty hands and faces, and your new dotted dresses!" she said. "Where have you been?"

Then Flicka, Ricka, and Dicka told her all about Aunt Helma.

Mother said quietly, "I have taught you always to help others. I am glad you were kind to Aunt Helma. You must be tired, so run along to bed. We'll do something about the dresses tomorrow!"

She caught them in her arms.

Early the very next morning the three little girls washed their socks and their new dotted dresses. Ricka mended her dress very carefully before she washed it.

"I'm sorry our red dotted dresses aren't new any longer," said Flicka.

"But Mother was glad we were kind and helpful," said Dicka.

"Our dresses will always be pretty," added Ricka. "I wonder how Aunt Helma will get along. She really needs our help."

Mother smiled as she overheard them. Then she said understandingly, "Always help others, every way you can. But when next you help Aunt Helma, why not wear your overalls?"

The three little girls washed their socks and their new dotted dresses.

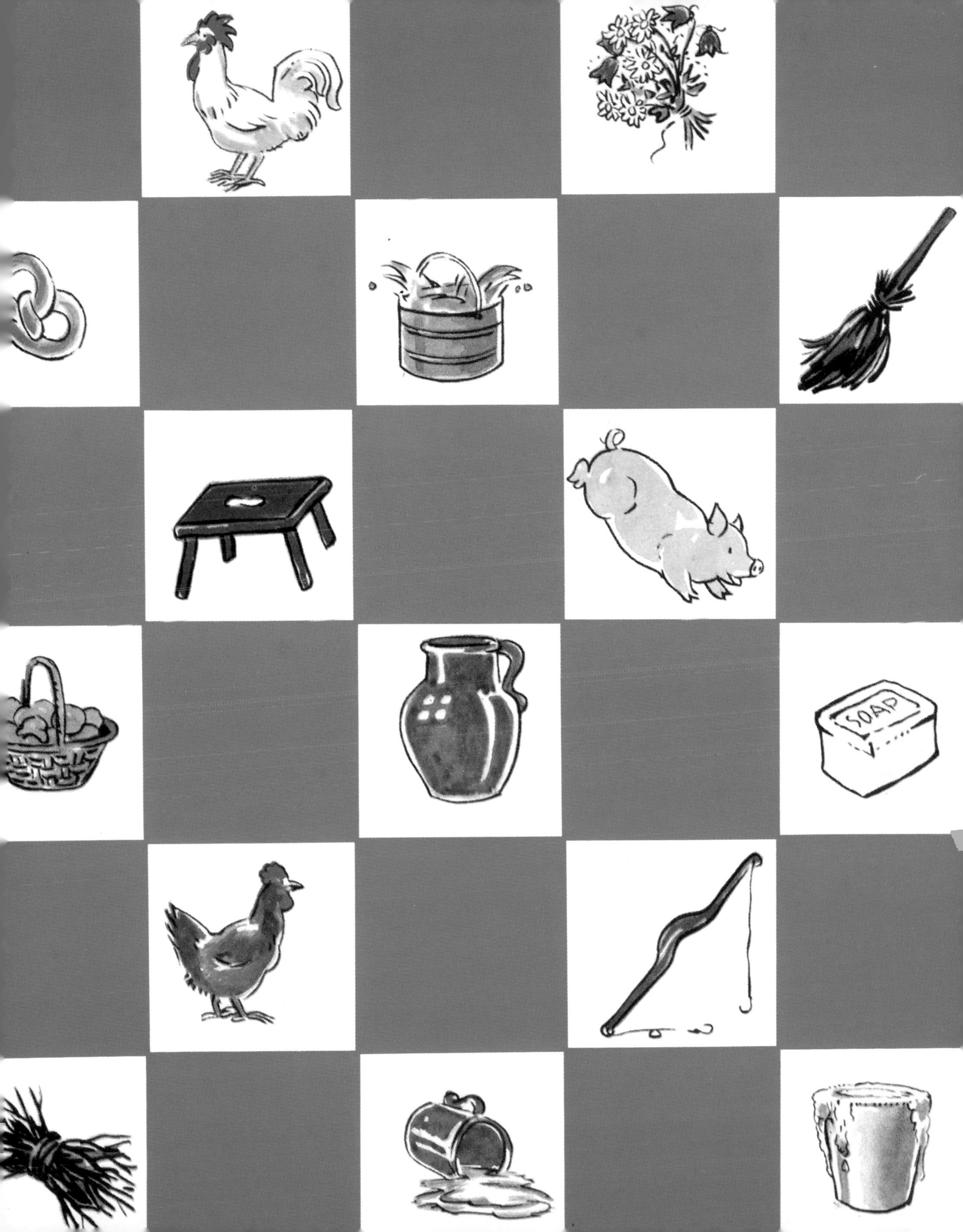
SOAP